Dedicated to

Gene Callaghan

1963 - 2017

"A Friend, a Brother, and a Dog Lover"

My name is James

and I know the
Goofiest Greyhound
in the world!!!!

I guess I should start at the beginning,
well I live with Susanne, Vincent,
and their adopted Son Frankie.

I had it made ,

all the attention
was on me!!!!

I had Frankie to myself,

the couch to myself,

and even the bed to myself!!!

Vincent and Susanne adopted her,
just like they did me and Frankie!!!!!

Now I had to share...

Frankie and my toys

The Couch

...and even my bed!!!!

She sat on the couch Goofy!!!!

Oh Savannah YOU ARE ONE GOOFY GREYHOUND!!

She plays with our toys GOOFY, she throws them in the air like she does not care.

She is so GOOFY
She eats Ice as if it were
a dog treat.

She is so GOOFY she doesn't even bark, unless Frankie teases her around the coffee table then she barks, but it's a GOOFY bark not like my fierce bark

Oh Savannah YOU ARE
      ONE GOOFY GREYHOUND!!!!!

When we go for a walk she gets all GOOFY and trys to pull Vincent in another direction,

Vincent calls her a stubborn old goat but I just call her GOOFY!!!

When we go for a walk she gets all GOOFY and trys to pull Vincent in another direction,

Vincent calls her a stubborn old goat but I just call her GOOFY!!!

She's so goofy she likes to wear hats, what respectable dog wears a hat?

Oh Savannah YOU ARE ONE GOOFY GREYHOUND!!!!!

You know what it's kind of fun knowing
a Goofy Greyhound!!!!

She kind of makes us all Laugh.
Eventhough she is GOOFY she is part of the
family and we wouldn't trade her for anything.

I guess I can call her my Goofy sister.

Next time I will tell you about the
        GOOFY adventures she has gotten me into,

Oh Savannah

YOU ARE ONE GOOFY GREYHOUND!

Savannah the Goofy Greyhound

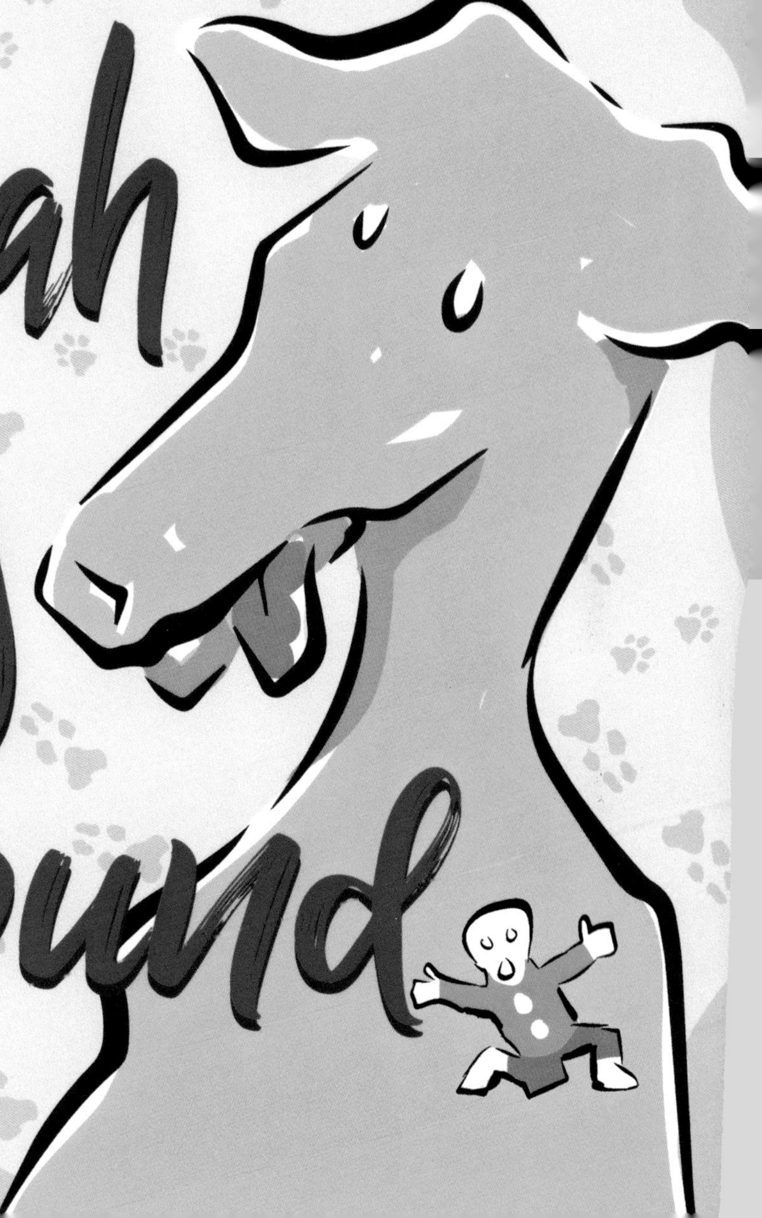

Michael V. Barry

is the Author of the
"Savannah the Goofy Greyhound" book.
He and his wife Mary Ellen
and their adopted son Donovan
live in a dog filled house
in Nashville, Tennessee.

The Barry family has opened their
house and rescued five dogs over the
past 10 years. The Barry's believe
you can rescue yourself by rescuing
others whether it is a dog or
it is a young boy or girl.
Rescue yourself today!!!!

Thomas McGrath

is the illustrator of the
"Savannah the Goofy Greyhound" book.

Thomas resides in West Chester,
Pennsylvania, with his lovely wife Krista
and three kids Tommy, Katie and Aidan.

Thomas is blessed to be a long time
friend and teammate to both
Michael and Gene.